W9-CDT-362

No Thanks,
but I'd Love to Dance

Choosing to Live Smoke Free

Jackie Reimer

In memory of Betty O'Mara-Skatchke

Published by the
American Cancer Society
Health Promotions
250 Williams Street NW
Atlanta, Georgia 30303-1002 USA

Manufactured by RR Donnelley
Manufactured in Reynosa, Mexico, in September 2009
Job# 76365

Printed in Mexico
5 4 3 2 1   10 11 12 13 14

Library of Congress Cataloging-in-Publication Data

Reimer, Jackie.
    No thanks, but I'd love to dance! : choosing to live smoke free/by Jackie Reimer.
        p. cm.
    "Originally published in 2008 by Jackie Reimer."
    ISBN-13: 978-1-60443-027-1 (hardcover : alk. paper)
    ISBN-10: 1-60443-027-3 (hardcover : alk. paper)
1. Smoking—Juvenile literature. 2. Smoking—Prevention—Juvenile literature.
3. Children—Tobacco use—Prevention—Juvenile literature. I. Title.
    HV5745.R42 2010
    613.85—dc22   2009028574

Originally published in 2008 by Jackie Reimer
Illustrated by Barry Cervantes

For more information about cancer, contact your American Cancer Society at **800-227-2345** or **cancer.org**.

For bulk sales, e-mail the American Cancer Society at trade.sales@cancer.org.

There once was a six-year-old girl named Annabelle. Everyone called her Belle.

Belle had a nice family and lots of friends, but her very best friend in the whole world was her Grandma Bee.

Belle and Grandma Bee did some very cool things together. They danced, which was Belle's favorite.

They played video games, which was Grandma
Bee's favorite.

They even played office together. Belle would seal the letters and put stamps on Grandma Bee's mail that needed to go to the post office.

Grandma Bee lived near Belle's house, so they spent almost every day together.

They had awesome tea parties with Grandma Bee's dog, Molly.

They drank real tea, had real cookies, and they even had real dog biscuits for Molly—that was Molly's favorite.

They were super-duper friends of the very
best kind.

One day when Grandma Bee and Belle were dancing, Grandma said, "Belle, I'm pooped. I have to sit down and rest."

Belle wondered why Grandma Bee was so tired.

Grandma Bee's doctor had told her that she was not getting enough oxygen from the air she breathed. He said she would need a tank filled with oxygen to help her breathe.

Grandma Bee explained to Belle that there is a gas in the air called oxygen. Our lungs take in oxygen when we breathe.

Oxygen gives our bodies what they need to turn food into energy, to keep our hearts beating, our brains thinking, and our bodies moving.

Grandma Bee told Belle she needed the oxygen tank because her lungs had been damaged from smoking when she was younger. She said, "Some people are born with weak or damaged lungs, and some people get damaged lungs just from doing their jobs."

"Like firemen?" Belle guessed.

"Yes, like firemen," Grandma answered.

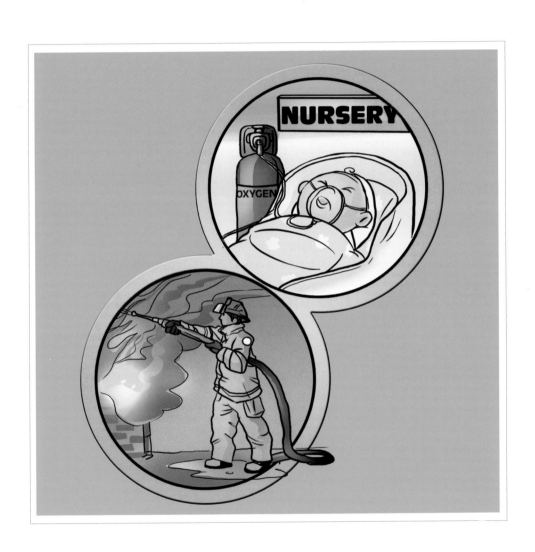

"I made the choice to smoke; that is why my lungs are damaged," said Grandma Bee.

"The smoke from tobacco can damage lungs in different ways. The damage makes it hard for oxygen to get into and out of the lungs. Without enough oxygen, we cannot do all the things we love to do."

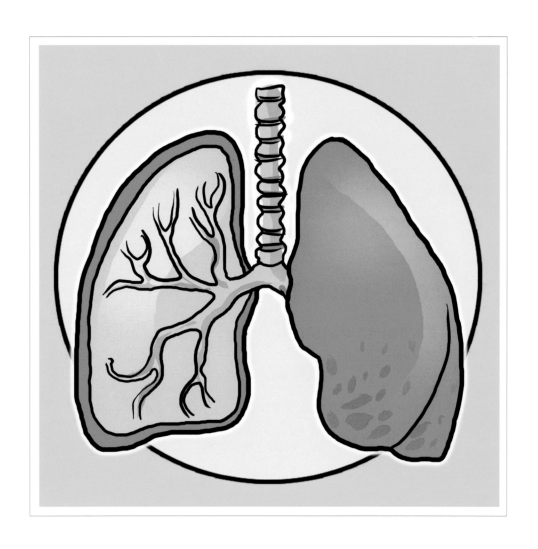

"Like dancing, Grandma?" asked Belle.

"Yes, Belle, like dancing!" responded Grandma Bee.

"But I LOVE, LOVE, LOVE, LOVE, LOVE to dance! I want to dance forever!" sang Belle.

Belle stopped dancing for a moment and asked, "Grandma, WHY did you choose to smoke?"

Grandma Bee told Belle her story. . . "It was a long time ago. I went to a dance with a boy. He was handsome and polite, and I thought he was the nicest boy I knew. After we danced and had some punch, we walked outside to get fresh air. Then he asked me if I would like a cigarette.

"Everyone was smoking, and they all looked so cool, just like in the movies, so I said 'yes.' It took only one cigarette for me to start smoking. But it took many, many years and many, many times to stop."

19

"Grandma, if you had never started smoking, you would not have had to try so hard to stop. Then you would be able to dance with me now without getting tired so fast," Belle said.

"Yes, it would have been much easier not to start smoking, Belle. It was a bad choice I made. I would have loved to dance some more instead."

"I know what you should have said when he asked you to smoke, Grandma!"

"You do?" asked Grandma Bee.

"YES!" Belle exclaimed. "You should have said, 'No thanks, but I'd LOVE to dance!!!' "

"Belle, you are so clever! I wish I had said that. At six years old, you are smarter than your Grandma Bee!"

"Molly doesn't smoke, so she's smart, too, Grandma!"

They laughed and laughed. Molly jumped up on the couch to join in the fun.

As the years passed and Belle got older, she went to high school; then she went to college. She had many jobs and made many friends. Some people would ask Belle if she would like a cigarette, or other things she knew were not healthy for her.

Whenever they asked her, Belle would think of Grandma Bee, smile, and say, "No thanks, but I'd LOVE to dance!"

About the Author

Jackie Reimer is a mother of two who loves to write and has a message to impart.

Her own mother's health was affected by making the choice to smoke. As a result, the quality of life with her grandchildren was also affected.

No Thanks, but I'd Love to Dance was written to give kids a ready-made response to offers of smoking.

Jackie lives in California with her husband, Ken; their daughters, Erica and Jordan; and their Chihuahuas, Bruno and Nora.

Other American Cancer Society Books for Children and Families

Available everywhere books are sold and online at **cancer.org/bookstore**

Because…Someone I Love Has Cancer: Kids' Activity Book

Cancer in the Family: Helping Children Cope with a Parent's Illness

Get Better! Communication Cards for Kids & Adults

The Great American Eat-Right Cookbook

Healthy Air: A Read-Along Coloring & Activity Book (25 per pack: Tobacco avoidance)

Healthy Bodies: A Read-Along Coloring & Activity Book (25 per pack: Physical activity)

Healthy Food: A Read-Along Coloring & Activity Book (25 per pack: Nutrition)

Healthy Me: A Read-Along Coloring & Activity Book

I Can Survive

Jacob Has Cancer: His Friends Want to Help

Kicking Butts: Quit Smoking and Take Charge of Your Health

Kids' First Cookbook: Delicious-Nutritious Treats To Make Yourself!

Let My Colors Out

Mom and the Polka-Dot Boo-Boo

Nana, What's Cancer?

Our Dad Is Getting Better

Our Mom Has Cancer (hardcover)

Our Mom Has Cancer (paperback)

Our Mom Is Getting Better